Allies

Adventures in the Liaden Universe®
#12

SRM Publisher, Ltd
Unity, Maine

Allies Copyright © 2006 by Sharon Lee and Steve Miller
Authors' website: http://www.korval.com

Allies
Published by SRM Publisher, Ltd.
PO Box 179
Unity, ME 04988

Editing by Steve Miller
Copyediting by Elektra Hammond

Cover Copyright © 2006
Cover design by Richard Horn
Second Life Snapshot by Elan Neruda

ISBN 0-9776639-4-9
ISBN 978-0-9776639-4-1
http://www.srmpublisher.com
First SRM Publisher, Ltd. edition: November 2006

Printed in the United States of America
0 9 8 7 6 5 4 3 2 1

Allies

Adventures in the Liaden Universe®
#12

Dedicated to the memory of

Don Miller,

who kept the cats and

never gave up dreaming

Fighting Chance

"Try it now," Miri called, and folded her arms over her eyes.

There was a couple seconds of nothing more than the crunchy sound of shoes against gritty floor, which would be Penn moving over to get at the switch.

"Trying it now," he yelled, which was more warning than his dad was used to giving. There was an ominous sizzle, and a mechanical moan as the fans started in to work–picking up speed until they was humming fit to beat and nor yet there hadn't been a flare-out.

Miri lowered her arms carefully and squinted up into the workings. The damn' splice was gonna hold this time.

For awhile, anyhow.

"Pressure's heading for normal," Penn shouted over the building racket. "Come on outta there, Miri."

"Just gotta close up," she shouted back, and wrestled the hatch up, holding it with a knee while she used both hands to seat the locking pin.

That done, she rolled out. A grubby hand intersected her line of vision. Frowning, she looked up into Penn's wary, spectacled face; and relaxed. Penn was OK, she reminded herself, and took the offered assist.

Once on her feet, she dropped his hand and Penn took a step back, glasses flashing as he looked at the lift-bike. "Guess that's it 'til the next time," he said.

Miri shrugged. The 'bike belonged to Jerim Snarth, who'd got it off a guy who worked at the spaceport, who'd got it from–don't ask don't tell. Miri's guess was that the 'bike's original owner had gotten fed up with it breaking down every third use and left it on a scrap pile.

On the other hand, Jerim was good for the repair money, most of the time, which meant Penn's dad paid Miri on time, so she supposed she oughta hope for more breakdowns.

"Must've wrapped every wire in that thing two or three times by now," she said to Penn, and walked over to the diagnostics board. Pressure and speed had come up to spec and were standing steady.

"My dad said let it run a quarter-hour and chart the pressures."

Miri nodded, saw that Penn'd already set the timer and turned around.

"What's to do next?" she asked.

Penn shrugged his shoulders. "The 'bike was everything on the schedule," he said, sounding apologetic. "Me, I'm supposed to get the place swept up."

Miri sighed to herself. "Nothing on tomorrow, either?"

"I don't think so," Penn muttered, feeling bad about it, though it wasn't no doing of his–nor his dad's either. Though some extra pay would've been welcome.

Extra pay was always welcome.

"I'll move on down to Trey's, then," she said, going over to the wall where the heavy wool shirt that served as her coat hung on a nail next to Penn's jacket. "See if there's anything needs done there."

She had to stretch high on her toes to reach her shirt– damn' nails were set too high. Or she was set too low, more like it.

Sighing, she pulled the shirt on and did up the buttons. If Trey didn't have anything–and it was likely he wouldn't–then she'd walk over to Dorik's bake shop. Dorik always needed small work done—trouble was, she only ever paid in goods, and it was money Miri was particularly interested in.

She turned 'round. Penn was already unlimbering the broom, moving stiff. Took a hiding, she guessed. Penn got some grief on the street—for the glasses, and for because of being so good with his figures and his reading and such which he had to be, his dad owning a mechanical repair shop and Penn expected to help out with the work, when there was work. Hell, even her father could read, and figure, too; though he was more likely to be doing the hiding than taking it.

"Seen your dad lately?" Penn asked, like he'd heard her thinking. He looked over his shoulder, glasses glinting. "My dad's got the port wanting somebody for a cargo crane repair, and your dad's the best there is for that."

If he could be found, if he was sober when found, if he could be sobered up before the customer got impatient and went with second best . . .

Miri shook her head.

"Ain't seen him since last month," she told Penn, and deliberately didn't add anything more.

"Well," he said after a second. "If you see him . . ."

"I'll let him know," she said, and raised a hand. "See you."

"Right." Penn turned back to the broom, and Miri moved toward the hatch that gave out onto the alley.

*

Outside, the air was pleasantly cool. It had rained recently, so the breeze was grit-free. On the other hand, the alley was slick and treacherous underfoot.

Miri walked briskly, absentmindedly surefooted, keeping a close eye on the various duck-ins and hiding spots. This close to Kalhoon's Repair, the street was usually OK, Penn's dad paying the local clean-up crew a percentage in order to make sure there wasn't no trouble. Still, sometimes the crew didn't come by, and sometimes they missed, and sometimes trouble herded outta one spot took up in another.

She sighed as she walked, wishing Penn hadn't mentioned her father. He never did come home no more except he was smoked or drunk. Or both. And last time–it'd been bad last time, the worst since the time he broke her arm and her mother–her tiny, sickly, soft-talking mother–had gone at him with a piece of the chair he'd busted to let 'em know he was in.

Beat him right across the apartment and out the door, she had, and after he was in the hall, screamed for all the neighbors to hear, "You're none of mine, Chock Robertson! I deny you!"

That'd been pretty good, that denying business, and for a while it looked like it was even gonna work.

Then Robertson, he'd come back in the middle of the night, drunk, smoked, and ugly, and started looking real loud for the rent money.

Miri'd come out of her bed in a hurry and run out in her shirt, legs bare, to find him ripping a cabinet off the wall. He'd dropped it when he seen her.

"Where's my money?" he roared, and took a swing.

She ducked back out of the way, and in that second her mother was there–and this time she had a knife.

"Leave us!" she said, and though she hadn't raised her voice, the way she said it'd sent a chill right through Miri's chest.

Chock Robertson, though, never'd had no sense.

He swung on her; she ducked and slashed, raising blood on his swinging arm. Roaring, he swung again, and this time he connected.

Her mother went across the room, hit the wall and slid, boneless, to the floor, the knife falling out of her hand.

Her father laughed and stepped forward.

Miri yelled, jumped, hit the floor rolling–and came up with the knife.

She crouched, the way she'd seen the street fighters do, and looked up–a fair ways up–into her father's face.

"You touch her," she hissed, "and I'll kill you."

The wonder of the moment being, she thought as she turned out of Mechanic Street and onto Grover, that she'd meant it.

It must've shown on her face, because her father didn't just keep on coming and beat her 'til all her bones were broke.

"Where's the money?" he asked, sounding almost sober.

"We paid the rent," she snarled, which was a lie, but he took it, for a second wonder, and–just walked away. Out of the apartment, down the hall and into the deepest pit of hell, as Miri had wished every day after.

Her mother . . .

That smack'd broke something, though Braken didn't find no busted ribs. The cough, though, that was worse–and she was spittin' up blood with it.

Her lungs, Braken'd said, and nothin' she could do, except maybe ask one of Torbin's girls for a line on some happyjuice.

The dope eased the cough, though it didn't stop the blood, and Boss Latimer's security wouldn't have her in the kitchen no more, which meant no wages, nor any leftovers from the fatcat's table.

Miri was walking past Grover's Tavern and it was a testament to how slim pickin's had been, that the smell of sour beer and hot grease made her mouth water.

She shook her head, tucked her hands in her pockets and stretched her legs. 'Nother couple blocks to Trey's, and maybe there would be something gone funny in the duct work he was too big to get into, but Miri could slide through just fine.

Even if there wasn't work, there'd be coffeetoot, thick and bitter from havin' been on the stove all day, and Trey was sure to give her a mug of the stuff, it bein' his idea of what was—

A shadow stepped out from behind the tavern's garbage bin. Miri dodged, but her father had already grabbed her arm and twisted it behind her back. Agony screamed through her shoulder, and she bit her tongue, hard. Damn' if she'd let him hear her yell. Damn' if she would.

"Here she is," Robertson shouted over her head. "Gimme the cash!"

Out of the tavern's doorway came another man, tall and fat, his coat embroidered with posies and his beard trimmed and combed. He smiled when he saw her, and gold teeth gleamed.

"Mornin', Miri."

"Torbin," she gasped—and bit her tongue again as her father twisted her arm.

"That's Mister Torbin, bitch."

Torbin shook his head. "I pay less for damaged goods," he said.

Robertson grunted. "You want my advice, keep her tied up and hungry. She's bad as her ol' lady for sneaking after a man and doin' him harm."

Torbin frowned. "I know how to train my girls, thanks. Let 'er go."

Miri heard her father snort a laugh.

"Gimme my money first. After she's yours, you can chase her through every rat hole on Latimer's turf."

"But she ain't gonna run away, are you, Miri?" Torbin pulled his hand out of a pocket and showed her a gun. Not a homemade one-shot, neither, but a real gun, like the Boss's security had.

"Because," Torbin was saying, "if you try an' run away, I'll shoot you in the leg. You don't gotta walk good to work for me."

"Don't wanna work for you," she said, which was stupid, and Robertson yanked her arm up to let her know it.

"That's too bad," said Torbin. "'Cause your dad here's gone to a lot a trouble an' thought for you, an' found you a steady job. But, hey, soon's you make enough to pay off the loan an' the interest, you can quit. I don't hold no girl 'gainst her wants."

He grinned. "An' you—you're some lucky girl. Got me a man who pays a big bonus for a redhead, an' other one likes the youngers. You're, what—'leven? Twelve, maybe?"

"Sixteen," Miri snarled. This time the pain caught her unawares, and a squeak got out before she ground her teeth together.

"She's thirteen," Robertson said, and Torbin nodded.

"That'll do. Let 'er go, Chock."

"M'money," her father said again, and her arm was gonna pop right outta the shoulder, if—

"Right." Torbin pulled his other hand out of its pocket, a fan of greasy bills between his fingers. "Twenty cash, like we agreed on."

Her father reached out a shaky hand and crumbled the notes in his fist.

"Good," said Torbin. "Miri, you 'member what I told you. Be a good girl and we'll get on. Let 'er go, Chock."

He pushed her hard and let go her arm. Expected her to fall, prolly, and truth to tell, she expected it herself, but she managed to stay up and keep moving, head down, straight at Torbin.

She rammed her head hard into his crotch, heard a high squeak. Torbin went down to his knees, got one arm around her; she twisted, dodged, was past, felt the grip on her shirt, and had time to yell before she was slammed into the side of the garbage bin. Her sight grayed, and out of the mist she saw a fist coming toward her. She dropped to the mud and rolled, sobbing, heard another shout and a hoarse cough, and above it all a third and unfamiliar voice, yelling–

"Put the gun down and stand where you are or by the gods I'll shoot your balls off, if you got any!"

Miri froze where she was, belly flat to the ground, and turned her face a little to see–

Chock Robertson standing still, hands up at belt level, fingers wide and empty.

Torbin standing kinda half-bent, hands hanging empty, his gun on the ground next to his shoe.

A rangy woman in neat gray shirt and neat gray trousers tucked tight into shiny black boots. She was holding a gun as shiny as the boots easy and business-like in her right hand. Her hair was brown and her eyes were hard and the expression on her face was of a woman who'd just found rats in the larder.

"Kick that over here," she said to Torbin.

He grunted, but gave the gun a kick that put it next to the woman's foot. She put her shiny boot on it and nodded slightly. "Obliged."

"You all right, girl?" she asked then, but not like it mattered much.

Miri swallowed. Her arm hurt, and her head did, and her back where she'd caught the metal side of the container. Near's she could tell, though, everything that ought to moved. And she was breathing.

"I'm OK," she said.

"Then let's see you stand up and walk over here," the woman said.

She pushed herself up onto her knees, keeping a wary eye on Robertson and Torbin, got her feet under her and walked up to the woman, making sure she kept outta the stare of her weapon.

The brown eyes flicked to her face, the hard mouth frowning.

"I know you?"

"Don't think so," Miri answered. "Ma'am."

One side of the mouth twisted up a little, then the eyes moved and the gun, too.

"Stay right there until I tell you otherwise," she snapped, and her father sank back flat on his feet, hands held away from his sides.

"Get behind me, girl," the woman said, and Miri ducked around and stood facing that straight, gray-clad back.

She oughta run, she thought; get to one of her hiding places before Torbin and her father figured out that the two of them together could take a single woman, but curiosity and some stupid idea that if it came down to it, she oughta help the person who'd helped her kept her there and watching.

"Now," the woman said briskly. "You gents can take yourselves peaceably off, or I can shoot the pair of you. It really don't matter to me which it is."

"The girl belongs to me!" Torbin said. "Her daddy pledged her for twenty cash."

"Nice of him," the woman with the gun said.

"Girl," she snapped over her shoulder. "If you're keen on going for whore, you go ahead with him. I won't stop you."

"I ain't," Miri said, and was ashamed to hear her voice shake.

"That's settled then." The woman moved her gun in a easy nod at Torbin. "Seems to me you oughta get your money back from her daddy and buy yourself another girl."

"She's mine to see settled!" roared Robertson, leaning forward–and then leaning back as the gun turned its stare on him.

"Girl says she ain't going for whore," the woman said lazily. "Girl's got a say in what she will and won't do to feed herself. Girl!"

Miri's shoulders jerked. "Ma'am?"

"You find yourself some work to do, you make sure your daddy gets his piece, hear?"

"No'm," Miri said, hotly. "When I find work I'll make sure my mother gets her piece. She threw him out and denied him. He's no lookout of ours."

There was a small pause, and Miri thought she saw a twitch along one level shoulder.

"That a fact?" the woman murmured, but didn't wait for any answer before rapping out, "You gents got places to be. Go there."

Amazingly, they went, Torbin not even askin' for his gun back.

"You still there, girl?"

Miri blinked at the straight back. "Yes'm."

The woman turned and looked down her.

"Now the question is, why?" she said. "You coulda been next turf over by now."

"Thought I might could help," Miri said, feeling stupid now for thinking it. "If things got ugly."

The hard eyes didn't change and the mouth didn't smile.

"Ready to wade right in, were you?" she murmured, and just like before didn't wait for an answer.

"What's your name, girl?"

"Miri Robertson."

"Huh. What's your momma's name?"

Miri looked up into the woman's face, but there wasn't no reading it, one way or the other.

"Katy Tayzin," she said.

The face did change then, though Miri couldn't've said exactly how, and the level shoulders looked to lose a little of their starch.

"You're the spit of her," the woman said, and put her fingers against her neat gray chest. "Name's Lizardi. You call me Liz."

Miri blinked up at her. "You know my mother?"

"Used to," Liz said, sliding her gun away neat into its belt-holder. "Years ago that'd be. How's she fare?"

"She's sick," Miri said, and hesitated, then blurted. "You know anybody's got work–steady work? I can do some mechanical repair, and duct work and chimney clearing and–"

Liz held up a broad hand. Miri stopped, swallowing, and met the brown eyes steady as she could.

"Happens I have work," Liz said slowly. "It's hard and it's dangerous, but I'm proof it can be good to you. If you want to hear more, come on inside and take a sup with me. Grover does a decent stew, still."

Miri hesitated. "I don't–"

Liz shook her head. "Tradition. Recruiting officer always buys."

Whatever that meant, Miri thought, and then thought again about Torbin and her father being on the loose.

"Your momma all right where she is?" Liz asked and

Miri nodded.

"Staying with Braken and Kale," she said. "Won't nobody get through Kale."

"Good. You come with me."

*

"Grew up here," Liz said in her lazy way, while Miri worked through her second bowl of stew. "Boss Peterman's territory it was then. Wasn't much by way of work then, neither. Me, I was little bit older'n you, workin' pick-up and on the side. Your momma, she was baker over—well, it ain't here now, but there used to be a big bake shop over on Light Street. It was that kept us, but we was looking to do better. One day, come Commander Feriola, recruitin', just like I'm doin' now. I signed up for to be a soldier. Your momma . . ." She paused, and took a couple minutes to kinda look around the room. Miri finished her stew and regretfully pushed the bowl away.

"Your momma," Liz said, "she wouldn't go off-world. Her momma had told her there was bad things waitin' for her if she did, and there wasn't nothin' I could say would move her. So I went myself, and learned my trade, and rose up through the rank, and now here I'm back, looking for a few bold ones to fill in my own command."

Miri bit her lip. "What's the pay?"

Liz shook her head. "That was my first question, too. It don't pay enough, some ways. It pays better'n whorin', pays better'n odd jobs. You stand a good chance of gettin' dead from it, but you'll have a fightin' chance. And if you come out on the livin' side of that chance, and you're smart, you'll have some money to retire on and not have to come back to Surebleak never again."

"And my pay," Miri persisted, thinking about the drug Braken thought might be had, over to Boss Abram's turf, that might stop the blood and heal her mother's lungs. "I can send that home?"

Liz's mouth tightened. "You can, if that's what you want. It's your pay, girl. And believe me, you'll earn it."

Braken and Kale, they'd look after her mother while she was gone. 'Specially if she was to promise them a piece. And it couldn't be no worse, off-world than here, she thought–could it?

"I'll do it," she said, sounded maybe too eager, because the woman laughed. Miri frowned.

"No, don't you spit at me," Liz said, raising a hand. "I seen temper."

"I thought–"

"No, you didn't," Liz snapped. "All you saw was the money. Happens I got some questions of my own. I ain't looking to take you off-world and get you killed for sure. If I want to see you dead, I can shoot you right here and now and save us both the fare.

"And that's my first question, a soldier's work being what it is. You think you can kill somebody?"

Miri blinked, remembering the feel of the gun in her hand–and blinked again, pushing the memory back away.

"I can," she said, slow, "because I have."

Liz pursed her lips, like she tasted something sour. "Have, huh? Mind sharing the particulars?"

Miri shrugged. "'Bout a year ago. They was kid slavers an' thought they'd take me. I got hold of one of their guns and–" she swallowed, remembering the smell and the woman's voice, not steady: Easy kid . . .

". . . and I shot both of 'em," she finished up, meeting Liz's eyes.

"Yeah? You like it?"

Like it? Miri shook her head. "Threw up."

"Huh. Would you do it again?"

"If I had to," Miri said, and meant it.

"Huh," Liz said again. "Your momma know about it?"

"No." She hesitated, then added. "I took their money. Told her I found the purse out behind the bar."

Liz nodded.

"I heard two different ages out there on the street. You want to own one of 'em?"

Miri opened her mouth – Liz held up her hand.

"It'd be good if it was your real age. I can see you're small. Remember I knew your momma. I seen what small can do."

Like whaling a man half again as tall as her and twice as heavy across a room and out into the hall . . .

"Almost fourteen."

"How close an almost?"

"Just shy a Standard Month."

Liz closed her eyes, and Miri froze.

"I can read," she said.

Liz laughed, soft and ghosty. "Can you, now?" she murmured, and opened her eyes, all business again.

"There's a signing bonus of fifty cash. You being on the light side of what the mercs consider legal age, we'll need your momma's hand on the papers."

*

Braken eyed Miri's tall companion, and stepped back from the door.

"She's in her chair," she said.

Miri nodded and led the way.

Braken's room had a window, and Katy Tayzin's chair

was set square in front of it, so she'd get whatever sun could find its way through the grime.

She was sewing–mending a tear in one of Kale's shirts, Miri thought, and looked up slowly, gray eyes black with the 'juice.

"Ma–" Miri began, but Katy's eyes went past her, and she put her hands and the mending down flat on her lap.

"Angela," she said, and it was nothing like the tone she'd used to deny Robertson, but it gave Miri chills anyway.

"Katy," Liz said, in her lazy way, and stepped forward, 'til she stood lookin' down into the chair.

"I'm hoping that denial's wore off by now," she said, soft-like.

Katy Tayzin smiled faintly. "I think it has," she murmured. "You look fine, Angela. The soldiering treated you well."

"Just registered my own command with merc headquarters," Liz answered. "I'm recruiting."

"And my daughter brings you here." She moved her languid gaze. "Are you for a soldier, Miri?"

"Yes'm," she said and stood forward, marshalling her arguments: the money she'd send home, the signing cash, the–

"Good," her mother said, and smiled, slowly. "You'll do well."

Liz cleared her throat. "There's a paper you'll need to sign."

"Of course."

There was a pause then. Liz's shoulders rose–and fell.

"Katy. There's medics and drugs and transplants–off world. For old times–"

"My reasons remain," Katy said, and extended a frail,

translucent hand. "Sit with me, Angela. Tell me everything. Miri–Kale needs you to help him in the boiler room."

Miri blinked, then nodded. "Yes'm," she said, and turned to go. She looked back before she got to the door, and saw Liz sitting on the floor next to her mother's chair, both broad, tan hands cupping one of her mother's thin hands, brown head bent above red.

*

Miri'd spent half her recruitment bonus on vacked coffee and tea, dry beans and vegetables for her mother, and some quality smokes for Braken and Kale. Half what was left after that went with Milt Boraneti into Boss Abram's territory, with a paper spelling out the name of the drug Braken'd thought would help Katy's lungs.

She'd gone 'round to Kalhoon's Repair, to say good-bye to Penn, and drop him off her hoard of paper and books, but he wasn't there. Using one of the smaller pieces of paper, she wrote him a laborious note, borrowed a piece of twine and left the tied-together package with his dad.

Liz'd told her she'd have a uniform when she got to merc headquarters, the cost to be deducted from her pay. For now, she wore her best clothes, and carried her new-signed papers in a bag over her shoulder. In the bag, too, wrapped up in a clean rag, was a smooth disk–intarsia work, her mother had murmured, barely able to hold the thing in her two hands.

"It was your grandmother's," she whispered, "and it came from off-world. It doesn't belong here, and neither do you."

"I'll send money," Miri said, looking into her mother's drugged eyes. "As much as I can."

Katy smiled. "You'll have expenses," she said. "Don't send all your money to me."

Miri bit her lip. "Will you come? Liz says—"

Katy shook her head. "I won't pass the physical at the port," she said, and coughed. She turned her head aside and used a rag to wipe her mouth.

She turned back with a smile, and reached out her thin hand to rest it on Miri's arm. "You, my daughter. You're about to begin the adventure of your life. Be bold, which I know you are. Be as honest as you can. Trust Angela. If you find love, embrace it."

The cough again, hard this time. Miri caught her shoulders and held her until it was done. Katy used the rag, and pushed it down beside her on the chair, but not before Miri saw it was dyed crimson.

Katy turned back with another smile, wider this time, and held out arms out. Miri bent and hugged her, feeling the bones. Her mother's lips brushed her cheek, and her voice whispered, "Go now."

And so she left, out the door and down the hall and into the street where Liz Lizardi was waiting, and the adventure of her life begun.

Prodigal Son

Miri, Val Con thought wryly as he moved silently down the pre-dawn hallway, *is not going to like this.*

He paused outside the door to the suite he shared with his lifemate, took a breath, and put his palm firmly against the plate.

The door slid aside, and he stepped into their private parlor, pausing just over the threshold.

Across the room the curtains had been drawn back from the wide window, admitting Surebleak's uncertain dawn. The rocking chair placed at an angle to the window moved quietly, back and forth, back and forth, its occupant silhouetted against the light.

"What ain't I gonna like?" she asked, apparently plucking the thought out of his head. Val Con shivered. The link they shared as lifemates made each aware of the other's emotions and general state of mind, and there had been instances of one of them suddenly acquiring a skill or a language which had previously belonged only to the other. This wholesale snatching of thoughts from his mind, though–that was new, and in one direction only. It seemed that Miri could read his mind perfectly well, while hers was as closed to him in detail as ever it had been. He wondered, not for the first time, if this was in some way linked to her pregnancy . . .

"Things looked kinda dicey there for a while," she went on. "From what I could tell."

"It was not without its moments," he allowed, moving toward the window. "Even the presence of Scout Commander ter'Meulen was insufficient to turn all to farce."

"If Clonak was half as stupid as he acts, something with

lotsa teeth would've had him for lunch a long time ago."

"True," he murmured from the side of her chair. He reached down and slipped his fingers through the wealth of her unbound hair. "But you discount the joy of the masquerade."

"No I don't. I just wonder why he bothers."

"I believe we must diagnose an excess of energy."

She snorted. Next to her, he smiled into the dawn, then sighed.

"Wanna tell me about it?"

"In fact," he said, dropping lightly to the rug beside her and leaning his head against her thigh; "I do."

"Ready when you are." He felt her hand stroke his hair and sighed in contentment made more poignant by the knowledge that it was to be all too brief.

"The highly condensed version," he murmured, "is that one of the teams the Scouts sent to gather the severed blossoms of the Department of Interior . . ." She choked a laugh, and he paused, his eyes on the meager garden below them.

"That's gotta be Clonak," she said.

"Indeed, Commander ter'Meulen was pleased to style it thus," he said. "Allow it, with the understanding that the actual business was not nearly so poetical."

He felt her hair move as she shook her head. "'Course it wasn't."

"Yes, well." Her robe was fleece, soft and warm under his cheek. "This team of Scouts obtained news of a situation which . . . lies close to us, cha'trez."

Her hand stilled on his hair. "How close, exactly?"

"Close as kin," he answered. "It would seem that the Department deployed a field unit, and perhaps a tech team, to Vandar after Agent sig'Alda failed them."

He felt her grasp it, and the frisson of her horror. Her

hand fell to his shoulder, fingers gripping.

"We gotta go in," she said, and he smiled at her quickness. "Zhena Trelu, Hakan, Kem–gods, what if they've already . . ."

"We have some hope that they have not already," Val Con murmured. "A field unit is by no means an Agent of Change. But we dare not tarry."

"We *are* going, then." There was satisfaction in her voice.

Val Con shook his head. "Alas, *I* am going. You, my lady, will stay here and mind Korval's concerns–and our daughter."

"Got a real hankering for a girl, doncha? What if the baby's a boy?"

"Then he will doubtless also be as intelligent and as beautiful as his mother."

Miri laughed, then sobered. "Who's your backup, then? If I'm staying home to mind the store."

"I thought to travel quickly," he murmured; "and leave within the hour. Clonak is gathering a contact team. He expects them to lift out no later than three days from–"

"What you're saying is that you're going in without any back-up." The rocker moved more strongly; inside his head, he heard the arpeggio of her irritation.

"Not," she said firmly, "on my watch."

"Cha'trez–"

"Quiet. I ain't gotta tell you how stupid it is to go into something like this by yourself, 'cause if you'd take a second think, you'd figure it out for yourself. What I am gonna tell you is you got two options: I go–or Beautiful goes."

He could not risk her–would not risk their child. His rejection was scarcely formed when he heard her sigh over his head.

"My feelings are hurt. But have it your way." Her hand left his shoulder. He rolled to his feet and helped her to rise, pulling her into an embrace.

"I will take Nelirikk with me," he whispered into her ear, and felt her laugh.

"That's a good idea," she murmured. "Glad you thought of it."

"Indeed." He hugged her tight, and stepped back. Slipping Korval's Ring from his finger, he handed it to her.

She shoved it onto her thumb and closed her fingers around it.

"Get your kit," she said. "I'll call down to the pilot and give him the good news."

*

It was a good thing, Hakan thought sourly, *that he'd come to university to study guitar.* The storm winds knew what they might have made him do, if he'd come to study walking. Lie on his stomach and march on his elbows, legs dragging in the dirt behind him, probably.

"Zamir Darnill," Zhena Teone, his music history professor, inquired crisply from the front of the classroom. "Is there a problem with your zamzorn?"

Besides it being the most useless instrument in the scope of creation? Hakan thought. A flute made from a full horn, with a range of only an octave, its point sharp enough to stab unwary fingers? No wonder the thing had been abandoned for the ocarina by the serious musicians of two hundred years ago. He sighed to himself and looked up.

"A little trouble with the fipple, Zhena," he said quietly. No matter his own feelings about flutes cut from ox horn, Zhena Teone doted on the thing; and if he'd learned nothing else at university thus far, he had learned that the wise student didn't provoke his professors.

"Zamir Darnill," his teacher said sadly. "The zamzorn represents an important part of our musical tradition. I fear you are giving it neither the respect nor the attention that it deserves."

"I'm sorry, Zhena," he muttered. "Flute isn't really my–"

"Flute? Flute indeed!"

Her pause was worth a fortune of concern, and when she spoke again it was obvious that she was keeping her voice level.

"Zamir, the king has seen fit to send you here, and you will have the goodness to learn. I suspect you have not been carrying the zamzorn on your person, as you have been told this last ten day, so that it stays at the proper temperature for playing at a moment's notice. In the past the only thing closer to a musical zamir than his zamzorn, was his zhena. So carry yours at all times, yes?"

She caressed the instrument in her hands, producing a subcurrent of stifled laughter in the room.

"You will have ample time to pursue your interest in stringed instruments–" she made it sound like a disease, or at least an unpleasant habit that shouldn't be mentioned in polite company– "after you have absorbed the lessons that history has to teach us. Now, then. Has your disagreement with the fipple been resolved?"

There was an outright titter from the front row, and Hakan felt his ears heat.

"Yes, Zhena."

"Good. I direct the class's attention once more to the jig on page forty-five . . ."

*

"A green and pleasant world," Nelirikk said, as they broke their march for the meal local time decreed as dinner. "Is it always so chill?"

"Never think it," Val Con answered. "In fact, I am persuaded there are those native to the world who would pronounce today balmy in the extreme, and perfect for turning the garden."

Nelirikk sipped from his canteen. He was, Val Con thought, a woodsman the like of which Gylles had rarely seen: bold in black-and-red plaid flannel, work pants, and sturdy boots, with a red knit cap pulled down over his ears in deference to the chill of dusk.

The big man finished his drink and resealed the jug. "This . . . error the captain sends us to correct," he began.

Val Con lifted an eyebrow. Nelirikk paused, and was seen to sigh.

"Scout, I do not say it was the captain's error."

"Nor should you," Val Con said, surprised by the edge he heard on his own words. He raised a hand, showing empty palm and relaxed fingers.

"The situation—which might, in truth, be said to be error—is of my crafting," he said, more mildly. "It was I who chose to land on an interdicted world. Saying that I did so in order to preserve the lives of the captain and myself does not change the decision or the act. Once here, we inevitably accrued debt, which must of course be Balanced. All of which is aside my decision to See Hakan Meltz. At the time, I stood as thodelm of yos'Phelium, so it was not a thing done lightly. And yos'Phelium abandons a brother even less readily than Korval relinquishes a child."

Nelirikk was sitting very still, canteen yet in hand, his eyes noncommittal. Likely he was astonished at such a rush of wordage. Val Con gave him a wry look.

"You see how my own stupidity rankles," he said. "I should at least have taken my boots off before leaping down your throat."

A smile, very slight, disturbed the careful blandness of Nelirikk's face.

"We have both made errors, I think," he said. "If ours are larger, or knottier, than the mistakes of the common troop, it is because our training has given us more scope."

Val Con grinned. *"Anyone may break a glass,"* he quoted. *"But it wants a master to break a dozen."*

There was a small silence while Nelirikk stowed his canteen.

"What I wondered," he said eventually; "is if we will be able to remove these infiltrators without raising questions in the minds of the natives. There are, so I'm told by the Old Scout, certain protocols for operations on forbidden worlds. If we simply eliminate the enemy . . ."

"If we simply eliminate the enemy, Clonak will have both of our heads to hang on his office wall," Val Con said. "No, I fear it must be capture and remove."

Nelirikk frowned, doubtless annoyed by such inefficiency. "If they've established themselves, any removal will cause comment among the natives," he pointed out.

"Indeed it will–and the least of the sins I must bear for choosing survival." Val Con stood and stretched. "If you are rested, friend Nelirikk, let us go on. Our target is only a short stroll beyond those trees."

*

The presentation was already underway by the time Hakan arrived at the Explorers Club. He slid into a chair in the last row, wincing when the point of the zamzorn he'd crammed into the inner pocket of his jacket jabbed him in the chest.

"Wind take the thing," he muttered, shifting. His chair lodged noisy protest, and the zhena beside him hissed, "Shhhhhh."

Hakan sighed and subsided. It wasn't bad enough that he was late for the meeting because of having to attend remedial class on the stupid thing, but now it was outright trying to kill him.

He tried to ignore his irritation and focused his attention on the front of the room. Tonight's lecture was entitled "The Future of Aerodynamics," a subject which at first glance seemed more alien to the interests of a guitarist than even the wind-blasted zamzorn. Hakan, however, had acquired an obsession.

Every free hour found him in the library, perusing the latest industry magazines and manuals. That a good deal of the information he read was so much noise to his untutored mind deterred him not at all. To the contrary, the realization that he had much to learn inspired him to begin attending an entry level aeronautics course, as an observer. He soon found that the acquisition of even the most basic concepts unlocked the meaning of some of what he continued to read.

Unfortunately, this heady taste of knowledge only made him thirstier.

He began to audit an advanced math class on his lunch hours, neglecting guitar while he stretched to encompass this new way of describing the world.

At mid-semester, frustrated by the slow place of the basic aeronautics course, he considered dropping music altogether and applying to the technical college. It was only the realization that he would have to explain his reasons to Kem that had, so far, deterred him.

It was at mid-semester, too, that Zhena Cahn, the

aeronautics instructor, called him to stay after class to talk with her–unprecedented for an observing student. And she had told him of the Explorers Club, and said that he might find the meetings of interest.

In fact, he had found them of interest. Even though he kept himself to the edges of the company during the social period, listening to the conversations of people much more learned than he; and even though almost half of the presentations were beyond him, he continued to go to the meetings, and to audit his extra classes.

Little by little, he began to understand, to grasp concepts, to extrapolate . . .

The zhena at the front of the room–he'd missed her name–was not a gifted speaker, but even her dry recitation could not close his mind to the marvels of jet-assisted flight, or heady imaginings of air speeds in excess of two hundred and fifty miles an hour.

All too soon, the zhena stepped down from the podium. The rest of the audience, held as rapt as Hakan, shifted, stood, and sorted out into separate human beings, each heading for the refreshment table.

As was his custom, Hakan took some cheese and a cup of cider–his dinner, this evening, thanks to the remedial session–and wandered the edges of the group, stopping now and then to listen, when an interesting phrase tantalized his ear.

He had almost completed his circuit, and was thinking, regretfully, that it really was time to be getting on home, when he caught the quick flicker of gold-toned fingers, deep toward the center of the crowded room.

His heart stuttered, then slammed into overtime. He put his cup and plate on the precarious edge of an overfull bookshelf, took a breath and dove into the crowd.

*

It was not quite full dark. Overhead, the few stars were dulled by a high mist. Val Con moved carefully, all-too-mindful of the guards–of the garrison!–nearby. His choice would have been to wait until the sluggish early hours for his infiltration. Alas, that he had no choice.

He'd left Nelirikk at the entry point, to stand as guard and watcher, under orders not to interfere with the soldiers' duty, unless their duty moved them to interfere with the captain's mission. His own progress was by necessity slow, as he wished to avoid not only discovery, but tripping over the odd spade, hoe, or burlap bag half full of manure. So far, he had managed well enough, but he could only guess at the perils which awaited him as he drew closer to the target.

The terrain had changed considerably since his last visit, and it was difficult to get his precise bearings. His internal map told him that he should be within a few steps of the scuppin house, though he neither saw–nor smelled–that structure. He did, however, blunder into the soft, treacherous footing of a newly turned garden patch.

He wobbled, and prudently dropped to one knee. It wouldn't do to call attention to himself, no–

But it appeared he had gained someone's attention after all.

Val Con kept himself very still as a shadow detached itself from the deeper shadows to his right, and moved toward him with deliberation.

*

"Borrill! Wind take the animal, where's he gone to now? Borrill!"

The old woman stood on the back step, staring out into the night. There were lights, of course, at the barracks and the guard stations, but she'd asked that her yard be kept more-or-less private, and they'd done as she'd asked.

With the result that it was black as pitch and her dog with his nose on a skevit trail, or, if she knew him, asleep in the newly turned garden patch.

"Borrill!" she shouted one more time, and listened to the echoes of her voice die away.

"All right, then, spend the night outside," she muttered and turned toward the door.

From the yard came the sound of old leaves crunching underfoot. She turned back, leaning her hands on the banister until, certain as winter, Borrill ambled into the spill of light from the kitchen door, his tail wagging sheepishly, a slim figure in a hooded green jacket walking at his side.

She straightened to ease the abrupt pain in her chest, and took a deep, steadying breath.

"Cory?" she whispered into the night, too soft for him to hear–but, there, his ears had always been keen.

He reached up and put the hood back, revealing rumpled dark hair and thin, angled face.

"Zhena Trelu," he said, stopping at the bottom of the stairs, and Borrill with him. "I'm sorry to come so late. We should talk, if you have time."

"Well, you can see I'm still up, thanks to that fool animal. Come along, the two of you and let an old woman go inside before she catches her death."

He smiled, and put his foot on the bottom stair. She stepped into the kitchen to put the kettle on.

"Where's Meri?" That was her first question after he'd closed the door and hung up his coat.

He turned to face her, green eyes bright. There was something . . . odd about him, that she couldn't put her finger quite on–not just the subtly prosperous clothes, or the relative neatness of his hair, something . . .

"Miri is at home, Zhena Trelu. She sends her love–and I am to tell you that we expect our first child, very soon."

She looked at him sharply. "You left her home by herself when there's a baby due? Cory Robersun, you put that coat right back on and–"

He laughed and held his hands up, like he could catch her words.

"No, no! She is surrounded by kin. My sisters, the zhena of my brother . . . Miri is well cared for." He grinned. "She would say, too well-cared-for."

Zhena Trelu snorted. "She would, too. Well, you tell her that I expect to have a visit from that baby, when she's old enough to travel."

Cory inclined his head. "I will tell her, Zhena Trelu."

The kettle sang and she turned to the stove, busy for the next few moments with the teapot. When she looked up, Cory was at the far side of the kitchen, inspecting the molding around the doorway.

He turned as if he felt her looking at him, and gave that strange heavy nod of his. "The King's carpenters, they have done well."

Zhena Trelu sighed and turned her back on him, pulling cups off the rack. "Put it back good as new," she said gruffly. Except the piano in the parlor wasn't the instrument Jerry had loved, Granic's books and old toys no longer littered the attic, the cup his zhena had made was smashed and gone forever . . .

"Sometimes," Cory said softly, "old is better."

The teapot blurred. She blinked, sniffed defiantly, and poured. He came to her side, picked up both cups, and carried them to the table. She turned, watching the slender back. New clothes were all very well, but the boy was still as thin as a stick.

"Hungry?" she asked. He glanced over his shoulder.

"I have eaten," he murmured, and pulled out a chair. "Please, Zhena Trelu, sit. There is something I must say to you, and some questions I should ask."

"Well, then." She sat. From the blanket by the corner of the stove came a long, heart-rending groan. Cory laughed, and sat across from her. He raised his cup solemnly, and took a sip. Zhena Trelu watched him, giving her own tea a chance to cool–and suddenly gasped.

"The scar's gone," she blurted, forgetting her manners in the excitement of finally putting her finger on that elusive difference.

Cory bowed his head gravely. "The scar is gone," he agreed. "I was . . . brought to a physician."

Hah, thought the old lady, lifting her cup for a cautious sip. She'd heard of skin grafting for burn victims; likely there was something similar for scars. New-fangled and expensive treatment, regardless. Well, maybe the hero money had paid for it. And none of that, judging from the level, patient look he was giving her, was what he wanted to talk to her about.

"All right," she said grumpily. "Out with it, if you've got something to say."

"You are well-guarded here," Cory began slowly. "That is good."

She opened her mouth, then closed it. *Let the boy talk, Estra.*

"It is good because there are some . . . people. Some people who are here, maybe, only because I– we–were here. It is possible that these people will wish to question those who gave us shelter. Who gave us friendship." He paused to sip some tea, then gave her a serious look.

"These people–they are not very careful. Sometimes, they hurt people, break things, when they ask questions." He tipped his head, apparently waiting for her to say something.

Zhena Trelu drank tea and reminded herself that, while Cory had always been a little odd, that had been due to his foreign ways. He wasn't crazy, or dangerous. Or at least, he hadn't been.

"I ask, Zhena Trelu," Cory murmured, apparently taking her silence for understanding. "Are there strangers in town? Who have perhaps come to Gylles for no apparent purpose, who have been–"

"There's Zhena Sandoval and her brother," she interrupted him. "Haven't talked to 'em myself, but–they'd fit your description. Both of 'em got more questions than a three-year-old, from what I've heard."

"Ah," Cory said softly. "And their questions are?"

She shrugged. "You'll want to see Athna Brigsbee for the complete rundown. She's talked with the boy–Bar, I think the name is. From what she told me, he was all over the map, wanting to know about the Winterfair and the music competition, Hakan Meltz and I forget whatall. Athna said she might've thought he was a reporter maybe out of Laxaco City, but turns out he didn't know anything about the invasion, or the King making half the town into Heroes."

Cory frowned slightly. "It is possible . . . I cannot be certain unless I speak to the zhena or her brother, myself."

Zhena Trelu considered him. "Are you going to do that? I thought you said they were dangerous."

He gave her a slight smile. "Bravo, Zhena Trelu," he murmured.

She glared. "What's that supposed to mean?"

He moved his shoulders, his smile more pronounced. "I said these people were . . . not careful. You make the leap to dangerous. Yes. These people are dangerous. The care you gave to us puts you in danger." He paused to finish his tea, and set the cup gently on the table.

"Another question, Zhena Trelu?"

"Why not?" she asked rhetorically. "There's plenty of tea in the pot."

That got her another smile. "The last one, I promise. Then I let you go to bed."

Behind them, Borrill gave up another groan. Cory laughed, and Zhena Trelu felt herself relax. She'd missed that laugh.

"So," she prompted him, grumpy in the face of that realization. "What's your last question?"

"I go by Hakan's house earlier, but it is locked; shutters closed."

"Tomas Meltz is at assembly–he's our alderman, remember?"

He nodded. "And Hakan?"

"Why, Kem and Hakan got married just after Winterfair," she said. "I'm surprised Kem didn't write to Meri about it. Very nice wedding. Hakan's aunt on his father's side stood up for him, since his mother's been gone these twenty years, poor thing. Kem was as proud as you can imagine, and the whole town was invited to the feast, after. Next morning, they got on the train to Laxaco."

"I see," Cory murmured. "Laxaco? This would be their . . . their . . . honey trip? That is good. So I should look for Hakan at Kem's house?" He pushed back from the table slightly.

"No." Zhena Trelu shook her head, and he stopped, eyes intent. "You should look for both of them in Laxaco City. They enrolled in university. Athna Brigsbee set it up for them. Got on the phone to the King's minister of something-or-other and came away with two scholarships. Kem is studying the teaching of dance, I think, and Hakan his music. Only thing Kem has to pay is their living expenses, same as she would here."

Cory frowned slightly, and she shivered, which might've been the breeze, except the new house was tight, and double insulated, too. The only breezes that got in nowadays were invited.

"Zhena Brigsbee," he said carefully. "She told the brother of Zhena Sandoval this? That she had arranged for Hakan and Kem–"

"Shouldn't be surprised," Zhena Trelu said drily. "You know Athna, Cory."

"Yes," he breathed, staring down into his empty cup.

"Yes," he said again, and looked up into her face. "Zhena Trelu, I thank you. Keep your guards close. I think Zhena Sandoval and her brother will soon be gone." He pushed his chair back and stood, she looked up at him. He looked serious, she thought. Serious and concerned.

"Going to Laxaco?" she asked.

"Soon," he answered, and came around the table, quick and light. "Keep safe," he murmured, and surprised her by slipping an arm around her shoulder. He gave her a quick hug, putting his cheek against hers briefly.

Then he was gone, walking light and rapid across the kitchen. He took his coat down from the peg and shrugged into it, bent to tug on Borrill's ears – "Good Borrill. You know me, eh?"

Zhena Trelu cleared her throat.

"Cory."

His hand on Borrill's head, he sighed, then straightened,

slowly, and turned to face her.

"Zhena Trelu?"

"What's the sense of telling me to keep those guards close when you got 'round 'em like they were sound asleep? If these folks are as dangerous as you say, then they'll get in just as easy."

He drifted a step closer, bright green gaze focused on her face. "You make leaps and bounds, Zhena Trelu," he murmured. "It sits on my head, that you must learn these things."

Whatever that was about, she thought, and sent him as sharp a look as she knew how.

"That doesn't go one step toward answering my question," she pointed out.

Cory's eyebrow slipped up a notch. "No, it does not," he said seriously. "The answer is that I think these people will be gone . . . one day, two days. You will get a letter, when they are no longer a . . . threat."

"Is that so? And who's going to take them away, exactly?" She frowned, an idea striking her. "Cory, there's a whole mess of the King's Guard right out there. Why not point these folks out, and let 'em clean house? They're bored here, poor boys. It'll be good for them to have something more exciting to do than watch over an old woman and her dog."

Cory tipped his head. "I would do this," he said slowly. "Were these people already . . . breaking things. They are . . . polite, for now. Better that they are asked, politely, to leave."

The boy wasn't making sense, she thought. Or he was and she was too tired and too old to follow. She shook her head. "Have it your way."

"Thank you, Zhena Trelu." He paused. "It would be better, maybe, not to tell your guards that I have been here."

She snorted; he inclined his head.

"Yes. Zhena Trelu, I ask your forgiveness."

She blinked. "My forgiveness? For what?"

"For bringing change to Gylles–and to Vandar. I should not have come here, and put a whole world into danger. Choices have consequences. I know this–and still I chose life over death, for my zhena and for me."

The smooth golden face was somber; his shoulders not quite level.

Tears started; she blinked them back, and held her hand out. He came forward and took it, his fingers warm.

"You made a good choice, Cory. This world's been changing for a long time. Would you believe I remember a time when the nearest telephone was right downtown at Brillit's?"

He smiled, faintly. "I believe that, Zhena Trelu."

"Well, good, because it's true." She gave his fingers a squeeze and let him go.

He went light and quiet across the room, opened the door–and looked at her.

"Sleep well, Zhena Trelu. We will bring our child to see you–soon."

The door clicked shut behind him.

*

He'd never gotten near enough to talk to the zhena with the quick golden hands, though he had learned her name from another in the ring of her admirers: Karsin Pelnara. The zhena, according to Hakan's informant, was newly arrived in Laxaco; her precise field something of mystery, though she appeared well-informed in a broad range of scientific topics. The forward-coming zamir wasn't able to tell Hakan where the zhena had arrived from, precisely, though he did know that she had been sponsored in to the Club by Zamir Tang.

Seeing that he had little chance of approaching the zhena

herself, Hakan had gone off in search of Zamir Tang, finding him in his usual place beside the punchbowl, engaged in a heated debate with two students Hakan recognized as seniors in the aeronautics college.

He'd hung on the edge of that conversation for a time, first waiting for Zamir Tang's attention, and then because he found himself caught up in the description of the challenges of building a proposed supersonic wind-tunnel, until a random remark recalled him to the hour.

Which was . . . late.

And later, still, by the time he had walked across the dark campus, only to find that the trolley to the married students' housing had stopped running hours before.

By the time he'd walked home, it was no longer late, but very early.

Kem, he thought, using his key on the street door, *is not going to like this.*

*

Nelirikk was not at his post

This was . . . worrisome.

Val Con stood very, very still, listening.

Breeze rattled branches overhead, and combed the moist grass with chilly fingers. Somewhere to the left, and not immediately nearby, a night bird muttered and subsided. From further away came the sound of measured steps along pavement–the garrison guard, pursuing his duty. Beyond that, there was silence.

"Ain't like him to just run off," Miri said quietly from just behind his right shoulder.

"Nor is it." His murmured agreement had been shredded by the chilly breeze before he remembered that Miri was not covering his offside, but minding the Clan's business on

Surebleak.

He took a careful breath, and brought his attention back to the night around him.

From the right–a soft moan.

Cautiously he moved in that direction, slipping noiselessly through a scrubby hedge. He dropped to one knee and peered about. To the left a drift of last year's leaves, crackling slightly in the breeze.

To his right a shadow leaned over another, and then straightened to an impressive height.

"Scout?" Nelirikk said, softly. "Is it well with the old woman?"

"Well," Val Con said, exiting the shrubbery and moving toward the second shadow, which remained unmoving on the ground.

"A watcher," Nelirikk said, as Val Con knelt down. "And an uncommonly poor one."

Val Con slipped a dimlight from his inner pocket and thumbed it on. The unconscious watcher was unmistakably Liaden; a red welt marred the smooth, golden brow. His hat had fallen off, freeing static-filled golden hair badly cut in imitation of the local style.

"How hard," Val Con asked Nelirikk, thumbing the dim off and slipping it away, "did you hit him?"

"Scout, I only spoke to him."

"Oh?" He sent a glance in Nelirikk's direction, but the big man's face was shadowed. "What did you say to him, I wonder?"

"Dog of a Liaden, prepare to die," Nelirikk said calmly.

Val Con bit his lip. Inside his head, he heard the music of Miri's laughter.

"I see. And then?"

"And then he most foolishly tried to escape me, tangled his feet in a root and fell, striking his head. The guard was at the far end of his patrol, or he could not have missed hearing it."

"Ah." Val Con sat back on his heels. "And his pockets?"

"Empty now. According to those protocols the Old Scout taught me, this person is a criminal many times over."

"As we are. However, our hearts are pure."

The Captain's aide felt no need to reply to this truth, instead stuffing the downed man's contraband into a capacious rucksack.

Val Con reached again into his inner pocket, fingered out an ampule and snapped it under the unconscious man's nose.

A gasp, a frenzied fit of coughing. The blond man jackknifed into a sitting position, eyes snapping open. He blinked at Val Con, flicked a look beyond–and froze, his face a study in horrified disbelief.

"Galandaria," he whispered hoarsely, his eyes still riveted on Nelirikk. ". . . an Yxtrang . . ."

"Yes, I know," Val Con said calmly. "He is sworn to my service, which may be fortunate for you, for he will not undertake to pull your arms off without an order from me."

The Liaden swallowed, painfully.

"What is your name and mission?" Val Con asked.

The man closed his eyes. Val Con waited.

"Technician Ilbar ten'Ornold," the Liaden said at last. "We are attached to the Uplift Team, dispatched to the area in order to ascertain if Rogue Agent Val Con yos'Phelium . . ." He opened his eyes with a knowing start.

Gravely, Val Con inclined his head.

"Val Con yos'Phelium, Clan Korval," he murmured.

"Pray forgive my omission of the courtesies."

Ilban ten'Ornold sighed.

"Field Agent san'Doval and yourself were sent to ascertain whether or not I had left anything of interest to the Department in Gylles," Val Con said, softly, in deference to the guard still walking his line.

"Yes."

Val Con paused, head to one side, studying the man's face.

"You will perhaps not have received recent news of the home world," he said. "The Department–"

"We had heard that headquarters had been destroyed. That does not mean the Department has been eliminated."

"Of course not," Val Con said politely, and stood, taking care to brush the leaves off the knees of his pants. "Nelirikk."

The Yxtrang stepped forward, flexing his fingers and shrugging the chill out of his shoulders.

Tech ten'Ornold jerked backward, feet scrambling for purchase in the dead leaves.

Val Con turned, as if to leave.

"No! For the– You cannot leave me to this! I–"

Val Con turned back.

"Lead us, quietly, to your base in Gylles," he said. "Or I will indeed leave you alone with this man."

Nelirikk paused, and gave the poor fellow a toothy predator's grin, perfectly discernable in the dark.

Ilbar ten'Ornold stared, as if he would keep him at bay with the force of his terror alone.

"I agree," he said hoarsely. "Now, for the love of the gods put me under your protection!"

Val Con looked to Nelirikk, who dropped back a step, with a wholly convincing show of reluctance.

"I accept your parole," Val Con told the tech. "Now, fulfill your part."

*

"The Explorers Club," Kem repeated, her voice calm and cold. Inwardly, Hakan cringed. He'd thought that telling the truth was the best thing to do, though the truth came perilously close to . . . the thing they didn't talk about. The very thing that Kem didn't want to talk about.

Now he thought that he should have lied; invented an impromptu jam session or something else more-or-less plausible that she could have pretended to believe.

"What," Kem asked coldly, "is the Explorers Club?"

He cleared his throat, looking around their cluttered parlor, brightly lit at this unhappy hour of the morning, and Kem sitting stiff and straight in the rocking chair they'd bought together at the campus jumble shop. She still wore the exercise clothes she favored when she practiced dance, and he wondered if she had worked at it all the time he was away, again.

"Would you like some tea, Kemmy?" he asked, which was cowardly, unworthy, and wouldn't work, anyway.

"I'm not thirsty, thank you."

Well, he'd known better.

"The Explorers Club, Hakan," she prompted, voice cold, eyes sparkling. She was, Hakan realized, on the edge of crying, and it was his fault. His fault, and Cory Robersun's.

He was, he thought, committed to the truth now. It seemed unfair that telling it was more likely to make her cry than the comfortable lie he'd been too stupid to tell.

"The Explorers Club," he said slowly, "is a group of people interested in technology and the . . . future. Of flight, mostly. But other things, too."

"Other things," came her over-composed voice, almost

sweetly. "Like brewed tea coming out of a flat wall? Or a doctor machine?"

The things she hadn't believed, when he'd told her. The things Cory'd told him nobody would believe. He'd thought Kem would be different; that she'd believe him because she believed *in* him.

"Like those," he said calmly, his hands opening almost as if he gifted her with the information. "Tonight's presentation was on jet-assisted flight. We don't have it yet, but the zhena thought we will, in ten years or less, traveling at speeds three or four times faster than the aircraft we have today–do you see what that means, Kemmy? At those speeds, Basil would only be a day away; Porlint, maybe two. The world would get smaller, but in a good way, we could–"

He stopped because her tears had spilled over.

"Kem–" Hakan dropped to his knees next to the rocker, and put his arms around her, half-afraid she would pull away. To his relief, she bent into him, putting her forehead against his shoulder.

"Kem, I'm so sorry," he whispered, stroking her hair. "I–the time got away from me. I was waiting for a chance to speak with the new zhena–"

In his arms, Kem stiffened, and Hakan mentally kicked himself.

Why couldn't you just stick with guitar, Hakan Meltz? he asked himself bitterly.

"Which zhena was that, Hakan?" Kem's voice wasn't cold any longer; it sounded small and tired.

He closed his eyes, and put his check against her hair. *Get this right*, he advised himself. *Or you'll regret it every day for the rest of your life.*

"A new member of the club. . . " he said carefully.

"She's from . . . away. Nobody seems to know where, exactly. I'm told she's very knowledgeable, and has a number of . . . creative ideas." Kem shivered, and he went on hastily. "I saw her tonight, and–Kem, she looks like Cory."

Kem pushed against him, and he let her go, though he stayed on his knees beside the rocker. She looked down into his face, hers white and wet and drawn.

"Is she Cory's sister, then?"

"I don't think so. When I say 'looks like,' I don't mean family resemblance–or I do, but not close family. More like a fifth or sixth cousin, maybe. She's got the same gold-tan skin–and she's just a tiny thing, not much taller than Miri, if at all. And when she talks, she moves her hands the way Cory and Miri did sometimes–you remember . . ." He moved his hands in a clumsy imitation of the crisp gestures their friends had used.

"I remember," Kem said quietly. "And you wanted to talk to this zhena."

"I wanted to ask her if she knew Cory," he said. "And I wanted to talk to her about–" he stumbled against the forbidden subject, took a breath and soldiered on. "I wanted to talk to her about that aircraft of his. If she's a countrywoman, and an engineer, she might know–it might . . . really exist," he finished, lamely.

There was a long silence during which Hakan found it hard to breathe, though he kept his eyes on hers.

When she finally, tentatively, raised her hand and smoothed his hair, he almost cried himself.

"Hakan," she whispered, "why are you . . . obsessed with these things? You're a musician, not an engineer."

"I think," he said unsteadily; "I think people can be more than one thing, Kemmy. Don't you?"

Another silence, with her hand resting on his shoulder. "I

don't know. Maybe they can." She took a breath. "Hakan."

"Kem?"

"I would like to go to the next meeting of the Explorers Club with you."

He stared up at her, chest tight. "I–sure. But I thought you didn't–"

"I'd like to meet to this mystery zhena," Kem interrupted. "If she does know Cory Robersun, I have a few things I want to say to her about him."

*

"The captain will have me shot," Nelirikk said, stubbornly.

He's said that once already today, but Val Con had dismissed it out of hand and continued preparations. Now, it needed to be addressed more forcefully since it was actually delaying lift-off.

"Indeed, she will not have you shot. Because, as we have discussed, you will begin calling for aid along our private channels the moment you clear far orbit, and you will not stop calling until you have raised either the captain herself, the elder scout, or Commander ter'Meulen. Once you have done this, you will report that the situation is far more complex than we had believed. That, in addition to no less than six field teams and four technical teams, there is at least one Agent of Change stationed in Laxaco City, whose intention is to speedily bring Vandar's technology to the point required by the new headquarters.

"You will report on your prisoners and their condition, and you will say that I have gone to Laxaco on purpose to ensure that Kem and Hakan Darnill are out of harm's way. I will attempt to locate the Agent, but I do not intend to confront such a one until I have substantial back-up."

"Yay!" Miri cheered in his ear. He ignored her.

"Scout–"

Val Con sliced the air with his hand, a signal for attention; Nelirikk subsided, though he dared to frown.

"If the captain has you shot, you have my permission to bludgeon me to death."

Nelirikk snorted. "A soldier's gamble, indeed." He sighed. "I will send back-up soon, Scout. Try not to do anything the captain would deplore in the meantime."

"It is my sole desire to behave only as the captain would wish."

"Pffft!" Miri commented, and even Nelirikk looked dubious.

But– "Safe lift, Scout."

"Fair journey, Nelirikk."

*

"There she is," Hakan whispered into Kem's ear, mindful of the zhena in the seat behind him. "She's sitting next to Zamir Tang–the man with the rumpled gray hair–in front of the pudgy man with the wispy mustache."

Kem took a good long look, her head tipped to one side. Hakan reached inside his coat and tried to adjust the zamzorn so its sharp end didn't pierce him through pocket, sweater and shirt. Wind, but he was going to be glad when the semester ended and he could put the stupid thing away forever or have it mounted as a trophy to his fortitude.

"I see her," Kem murmured. "She does look like Cory, doesn't she? In fact . . ." Her voice drifted off, and she frowned.

"What?" Hakan asked, forgetful of his voice, which earned him an emphatic *sssshhh!* from the zhena behind.

"What?" he whispered.

"Do you remember after the invasion, when Cory went off his head?"

Allies

As if he'd forget it soon. Hakan nodded.

"Zhena Pelnara reminds me of him like that," Kem whispered. "I can't quite–"

"If the pair of you don't have any interest in this presentation," the zhena in back of them interrupted in a hoarse whisper, "there are those of us who are."

Hakan looked at Kem. She was biting her lip, her eyes dancing. He grinned and secretly reached down between their seats and slipped his fingers through hers. She squeezed his hand, and he settled back, happier than he had been in many a month. Not even the zamzorn's prick against his ribs cast a shadow on his mood.

*

Val Con relaxed into the shadows across from the slightly seedy shingled building, the legend *Explorers Club* blazoned in bright yellow letters over the door. He had done a quick check of the building, looking for alternate exits, of which there was only one, and that one locked tightly. Not that a lock would necessarily stop, or even slow an Agent of Change, but Val Con rather thought she would be exiting by the front door, doubtless on the arm of the untidy old gentleman who had escorted her inside.

The Agent, Karin pel'Nara, if the records he had copied were accurate, had been busy this last while, sowing her seeds of forbidden tech in the most fertile ground available to her: the inventors, visionaries and crackpots associated with the greatest university in Bentrill. That she appeared for the moment to be concentrating her efforts in Bentrill was a comfort, though a small one. At least Clonak and the hopefully substantial mop-up team would have a relatively small segment of the world's population to deal with.

On the other hand, the Agent had been thorough, to the

point where Vandar might not be recoverable. Val Con sighed. The Department's philosophy regarding young societies had always been one of aggression and exploitation. The death of a few barbarians; the destruction of unique cultures; the upset of societies; or the death of entire worlds–none could be allowed to weigh against the Mission.

Well. It was hoped that Clonak arrived soon. A final determination of Vandar's status could certainly not be made until the pernicious influence was removed.

And, truth told, the Agent's influence was hardly any worse than his own in allowing a native of an interdicted world onto a spacecraft, in telling him things no man of his world and culture had need of.

Val Con sighed again, quietly.

He had tracked down both Hakan and Kem and assured himself of their continued good health. Indeed, it was the need to be certain that they had not fallen under the eye of Agent pel'Nara that had prompted him to infiltrate the Agent's base and copy those very revealing files.

Seeing that Kem and Hakan had not come into the Agent's circle, he had reconsidered his own plan to visit them and drop a word of warning in their ears. Better not to take the chance, in case the Agent were after all aware of his presence and interested in his movements.

The breeze freshened, rattling the handbills nailed to the post he leaned against. He wondered, idly, how long the Explorers Club would meet.

He was considering the advisability of moving closer when two figures came 'round the corner, moving quickly, their footsteps noisy on the cobbled walk. Latecomers to the meeting, Val Con thought–and then came up straight in his hiding place.

For the two latecomers were Hakan and Kem. As he watched they jogged up the sagging wooden stairs and disappeared into the depths of the Explorers Club.

Oh, Val Con thought. *Damn.*

*

The pattern of the last meeting held; after the presentation Zhena Pelnara was immediately surrounded, and there was no getting near her.

"She certainly is admired," Kem said, as they helped themselves to cider and cheese. "How long has she been a member?"

Hakan shrugged. "According to Zamir Fulmon, the zhena was sponsored into the club during the mid-course tests, and scarcely missed a meeting until she was called away on business. The last meeting was her first in some time. I didn't have time to attend meetings during the tests–which is why I'd never seen her before."

"Has she done a presentation?" Kem wondered. "What's her specialty?"

"I don't know," Hakan said. "We could check the event book."

"Maybe–no, look. She's leaving."

It did seem as if the zhena was taking leave of her friends. Zamir Fulmon, Hakan's informant of the last meeting, brought her coat and held it for her. The man with the odd mustache stood with two drinks in hand, as if he'd brought her one and been overlooked. Another zamir made an offer of escort, but she declined.

"No, it is kind of you, zamir, but I will meet my brother only a step down the walk. Stay, and continue this excellent conversation! Next meeting, I will want to hear how you have come to terms with this conundrum!"

She moved firmly toward the door, and the group stood aside to make way for her. Kem grabbed Hakan's arm and pulled him with her, heading for the door the long way, around the edge of the crowd.

"What–?" he managed, as they reached the vestibule, coats flapping open in their haste.

"Let's try to overtake her on the walk," Kem said. "It will be a perfect chance to ask her about Cory!"

*

Someone, Val Con was certain, was watching him–and had been for some time. There was no overt evidence to support this certainty, which only meant that whoever it was, they were very good. He didn't believe it was Agent pel'Nara, though it certainly could be one of her team, assigned as back-up.

He considered wandering away, to see whether the watcher would follow, but that would mean leaving Hakan and Kem in the Agent's orbit without back-up. Though what he might do if the three of them emerged arm-in-arm from the–

The door to the Explorers Club opened and Agent pel'Nara stepped out, alone, pulling on her gloves as she descended the tricky stairs. Apparently his friends had no need of his protection this evening. It galled him to let Agent pel'Nara go, but he judged that prudence would counsel him to walk away in a moment or two, and lose his watcher in the narrow streets to the west of the campus. He could always find the Agent again, tomorrow.

Agent pel'Nara was almost to the walkway. The door to the Explorers Club opened again, spilling Hakan and Kem into the night.

Val Con froze.

Agent pel'Nara, apparently oblivious, strode steadily down the walkway toward his position. Kem clattered down the last few steps and hit the walk very nearly at a run, Hakan lagging behind.

"Zhena Pelnara!" she called.

The Agent checked, then turned, head cocked to one side.

"Zhena?" she said politely, as Kem came, breathlessly, to her side. "I am not aware of your name, I think?"

"Kem Darnill. I was at the meeting. I'm sorry to chase you down like this, but it was impossible to get near you at the reception."

"Ah," Agent pel'Nara said indulgently. "You have an idea, perhaps? A theory? But you must return and share it with the others. It is with sadness that I must leave early, but–I have an appointment, zhena. Good-night."

She turned, and Val Con dared to hope that the encounter was over. Kem, however, was not to be put off.

"I don't have an idea," she said, "but a question. It will only take a moment, zhena."

Agent pel'Nara was seen to sigh. She turned back. "Very well," she said, her voice a little impatient now. "But quickly if you please, Zhena Darnill."

Kem smiled as Hakan came up next to her. "This is my zamir, Hakan," she said to the Agent. "We both noticed you in the meeting. You look very much like a friend of ours . . . from . . . away."

The Agent's stance changed; she was no longer poised to walk away. She was, Val Con saw, *interested* in this. As well she might be.

"I am intrigued, zhena," she said; "there are very few of my–of us in Laxaco City. What is your friend's name?"

"Corvill Robersun," Kem said.

Val Con closed his eyes, briefly.

"Corvill Robersun," the Agent repeated, caressingly. "Now, Zhena Darnill, I must tell you that I do not know Zamir Robersun, myself. His work, though–that I know well. Do you say that he is in Laxaco? I will ask you for an introduction."

"Cory and his zhena went back home," Kem said seriously. "We'd hoped that you might have word. Also–"

"Do you happen to know–" that was Hakan, speaking quickly, his words all but stumbling over each other. "You said you knew his work . . ." He stopped, apparently embarrassed at having broken into the zhena's discussion.

Agent pel'Nara turned her attention to him. "I do indeed know his work, Zamir Darnill. What is it you wish to ask?"

"He had an . . . an aircraft, he called it," Hakan said, more slowly now, as if he dreaded the answer his question might earn, now that he was committed to asking it. "It wasn't . . . it didn't have a propeller, and there were other things kind of odd about it. But the oddest thing was that it lifted straight up. I saw the snow, and there were–"

"Who's there?" Kem said sharply.

"I hear nothing," Agent pel'Nara said soothingly, but Val Con, at least, knew she was lying.

The watcher was moving, stealthy and almost silent. Moving toward the threesome on the walkway.

Almost unbidden, Val Con found himself falling back into agent training and called up the decision matrix he knew as The Loop. Yes, there it was, the question of what an agent should do in this situation . . . and the probability that the watcher was going into an attack mode was close to unity.

Val Con's reaction was just as certain. Necessity existed.

Carefully, he bent and slipped the knife out of his boot, pausing to listen to the watcher's progress. Then, moving with considerably less noise, he charted an interception course.

*

The zhena's face had gone frighteningly, familiarly blank, as if she read some inner dialog.

It seemed to Hakan as if time suddenly speeded up. He felt a surge of adrenalin.

There was a crashing, a shout, from the small dark park beyond them. Zhena Pelnara reacted by reaching out and grabbing Kem's arm, simultaneously reaching inside her coat.

Kem twisted, broke free, and Hakan leapt, spinning behind the zhena, and his left arm was around her upper arms, pinning them, while his right hand held the sharp point of the slick horn zamzorn firmly against her throat.

The zhena relaxed slightly, as if recognizing and submitting to peril, and Kem dodged in, snatching something from the zhena's hand, and dodged back, holding the odd-shaped object uncertainly.

"That is not a toy, zhena," Karsin Pelnara said, her voice perfectly matter-of-fact. "Please have your zamir release me."

Hakan saw Kem adjust what she held, as if determining what it was, how to use it . . . and then she held it, surely, as if it were a tiny gun.

"Kem," a familiar voice, slightly breathless said from the suddenly silent park. "Please be very careful. The zhena is correct; that thing is not a toy. Hakan–"

Cory stepped out onto the walk, hair rumpled and coat torn, the knife he used against the invasion force–or its twin–in his left hand. It looked quite as it had during the invasion, too, with its shine mottled with fresh blood.

"Hakan, I will ask you also to be very careful. You have not finished your training with that . . ."

The woman in his grip twisted suddenly, a move Hakan

reacted to with his guardsman training. She redoubled her efforts, snarled, and bit at his hand holding the the instrument to her neck. He tried to pull away and the zamzorn slipped and clattered on the cobbles as it fell. Zhena Pelnara kicked, as the move required, but he'd moved and she missed, and spun her attention on Cory, who had dropped into a crouch, knife ready.

"Stop!" Kem shouted, and simultaneously there was a strange coughing sound, followed by the ring of metal on stone.

Zhena Pelnara stumbled–and collapsed to the cobbles at Cory's feet. He knelt down and turned her over, fingers against her throat a hands-breadth above a small stain on her blouse front.

"Did I kill her?" Kem asked, her voice unnaturally calm.

"No," Cory said shortly. "It is a . . . hypnotic . . . a sleep dose. She will rise eventually." He sighed then and said "The man in the woods, he was not armed with such a benign device, I think, and is not so lucky."

"Hakan, we will need something –a rope, a scarf, to tie her before–"

Very close, someone cleared his throat. Hakan jumped, and then relaxed as the pudgy man in a well-worn jacket smiled at him.

"Peace," he said, his words barely intelligible. "A friend of Cory, me."

Cory sat back on his heels and looked at the man over his shoulder. "You took your time," he said, crankily, to Hakan's ear. "Binders?"

"Right here," the pudgy man with the wispy mustache said, and knelt down beside him, adding, "Had you come inside, you might have found me an hour ago, you know, before I had to sip any of that treacly punch they expected us to drink . . . ."

*

Hakan was wide-eyed, and Kem no less so. Val Con leaned back in his chair and let them think it through. At the far end of the table, Clonak fiddled with his note taker, though Val Con was willing to bet there was nothing in the least wrong with it.

"Let me understand this," Hakan said finally. "You, and Clonak, and Zhena Pelnara, and—you're all from *another world.* And Zhena Pelnara broke some kind of law about leaving . . . worlds . . . like Vandar alone, and now there will be . . . *mentors* here to guide us . . . into the *next phase.* And you want *me* to be the go-between— between the mentors and the King, or the assembly or—whoever."

"That's right." Val Con smiled encouragingly. "I know we give you a lot of information, very quickly. If you agree, we can teach you—and you can teach us."

Hakan took a breath, eyes bright.

"He wants it," Miri commented.

"I—" Hakan started, glanced at Kem, then back to Val Con. "Why me?"

"Good question. Because already you have seen the impossible, already you . . . stretch and accept new ideas. Also, you act quick and with decision. Not many people could have surprised that zhena, or held her for so long." He, too, glanced at Kem, noting the tightness of her shoulders, the forcibly calm expression and the eyes bright with tears.

"Kem, you also make a quick decision—to take that weapon, to use it. It is well. This will not be so strange for you—already you are a teacher."

Her face relaxed slightly, though her eyes still swam.

"We'll have to talk it over," she said, sending a look to

Hakan. He nodded.

"Yes," Val Con said. "But not too long. I am sorry, but work must start–soon." He rose, gathering Clonak with a glance. "We leave you for an hour. Then we come back and you tell us what you decide."

"Lunch," Clonak added, "comes to help thought." He left the room, presumably to order lunch, and Val Con turned to follow him.

"Cory."

He stopped, and turned toward her. "Kem?"

"That aircraft Hakan told me about, with the tea that's brewed inside the wall, and the doctor machine you slide people into?"

"Yes."

"Is that really true?"

"Yes," Val Con said gently. "It is really true. And if Hakan wishes it, he may be taught to fly–not that craft, but one like it. You both might, if you wish."

"Wants that, too," Miri observed.

Val Con smiled. "That is for the future. For now, you decide the future."

As Val Con turned, Hakan said something quiet to Kem that sounded like, "We may wish to be two things, I think . . ."

*

He paused outside the door to the suite he shared with his lifemate, took a breath, and put his palm firmly against the plate.

The door slid aside; he stepped into their private parlor– and stopped.

Across the room, the curtains had been drawn back from the wide window, admitting Surebleak's uncertain dawn. The rocking chair placed at an angle to the window moved quietly, back and forth, back and forth, its occupant silhouetted against the light.

"Took your time," Miri said.

He smiled and moved across the room, dropping to his knees by her chair and putting his head in her lap.

"I am glad to be home, too, cha'trez."

She laughed, her hand falling onto the back of his neck, fingers massaging gently.

"Emerging world, huh? Pretty slick way of doing things, Scout Commander."

"It was the only possible solution," Val Con murmured. "Hakan and Kem will do well, I think, as planetary liaisons."

"I think so, too."

"Also, we are to take our child to make her bow to Zhena Trelu, when she is old enough to travel safely."

"Be glad of the vacation," she said. "You don't mind my saying so, you could use some sleep. No need to rush back so fast."

"I did not wish to miss the birth of our daughter," he said, drowsy under her fingers.

"Not a worry. Priscilla says day after tomorrow."

"So soon?"

She laughed, and pushed him off her lap. He made a show of sprawling on the rug, and she laughed again, pushing against the arms of the chair.

Val Con leapt to his feet and helped her rise.

"I believe I will have a nap," he said. "Will you join me?"

"Wouldn't miss it for anything."

About the Authors

Sharon Lee and Steve Miller are the celebrated co-authors of the best-selling Liaden Universe® series and have been writing together since the first "Kinzel" stories hit *Fantasy Book* in the early 1980s. They started the first Liaden story in 1984 and have published a dozen novels and several dozen short works in that series alone. Along the way they've become fan favorites at SF conventions from California, USA to Fredericton, Canada, with Guest of Honor and Special Guest appearances at PenguiCon, COSine, AlbaCon, Trinoc*con, ConDuit, MarsCon, ShevaCon, BaltiCon, PortConMaine,SiliCon, Second Life Library, and elsewhere.

They count Meisha Merlin, Ace Books, Phobos, and Buzzy Multimedia among their English language publishers and have several foreign language publishers as well. Their short fiction, written both jointly and singly, has appeared in *Absolute Magnitude, Catfantastic, Dreams of Decadence, Fantasy Book, Such a Pretty Face, 3SF,* and several incarnations of *Amazing.*

Their work has enjoyed a number of award nominations, with *Scout's Progress* being selected for the Prism Award for Best Futuristic Romance of 2001 and *Local Custom* finishing second for the same award. *Local Custom* was published by Buzzy Multimedia as an audio book read by Michael Shanks - StarGate's Daniel. *Balance of Trade*, appeared in hardcover in February 2004 and hit Amazon.com genre bestseller lists before going on to win the Hal Clement Award as Best YA Science fiction for the year. Their most recent Liaden novels are *Crystal Soldier* and *Crystal Dragon* - and as usual they have a book due out in the spring.

More: Steve was Vice Chair of the Baltimore in 80 WorldCon bid as well as Founding Curator of Science Fiction for the University of Maryland's SF Research Collection, while Sharon has been Executive Director, Vice President, and President of the Science Fiction Writers of America; together they were BPLAN Virtuals, an ebook publisher in the late 1980s. These backgrounds give them a unique perspective on the science fiction field.